Merry Christmas!

KNOCK!
KNOCK!

Santa
Paws

Bobby was busy unwrapping a box,
When he heard the urgent-sounding knocks,
He stopped his mischief to open the door
And found there a reindeer, looking quite sore.

"I'm Rudolph," said the deer.
"Recognise the nose?
It shines a bright red
whenever it snows.

Santa's sleigh crashed!
It could be a lost cause...
Unless you can help
with your puppy paws?"

Outside, a plump figure lay on the ground,
Making a sobbing un-Santa-like sound.
"I'm crying," he said, "what else can I do?
We fell from the sky, lost all of our crew."

His superpower being doggy affection,
Bobby licked Santa's nose to regain his direction.
"Of course, dear pup, we can't give up now!
We must save Christmas, the question is how?"

The clever pup worked on releasing the sleigh
By digging and shoving the packed snow away.
But who would pull it? Santa needed his crew,
And this time, only a dog's nose would do.

Bobby sniffed the cold air and caught a scent,
Then into the shrubbery that puppy went.

He found Dasher struggling, caught in a bush
And got her out with a pull and a push.

"Thank you!" said Dasher. "But where is the sleigh?
We must place the presents before the big day!"
How would Santa do it with only two deer?
Seven were still missing – oh dear, oh dear!

Clever young Bobby had found the answer
To the whereabouts of nimble Dancer.

Having fallen through the roof of a cosy chalet,
She was treating two cats to their own private ballet.

"Come on now, Dancer, no time to delay!"
said Rudolph, as Dancer performed a plié.

Bobby had already caught the next trace
And wagging his tail, he picked up his pace.

Prancer and Vixen were riding the breeze
Using their reins for a bit of trapeze.

Next up was Cupid, who was feeling quite woozy,
After falling headfirst into a hot jacuzzi.

The clock was ticking, it would be Christmas Day soon.
Then Bobby's ears pricked at a familiar tune.

Someone was singing a sad Jingle Bells.
He sniffed the air – there were so many smells!

Comet had landed with Santa's supplies,
But she stopped her snacking to stare in surprise.
"Bobby from the Bin? The pup from the trash?
Have you come to the rescue after the crash?"

Though Bobby accepted a well-earned treat,
There wasn't the time to sit down and eat.
Donner and Blitzen were still to be found;
Everyone was panicking, looking around.

Santa was running this way and that,
His boots thumping, his hand on his hat.
"Oh, Bobby, dear Bobby, what shall we do?
The sleigh won't fly without the missing two!"

Just when they thought they had left it too late,
They saw Donner on ice, trying to skate.
Slipping and sliding, young Bobby went after
That clumsy deer, who was roaring with laughter.

With Donner on firm ground, Santa let out a sigh.
"If we don't find our Blitzen, again I will cry."
"Up here!" a voice called. "I seem to be stuck."
It looked like Blitzen had had some bad luck.

Squeezed into a chimney high on a roof,
The reindeer waved down with her heavy hoof.
"You need some butter to help you slide through,"
Rudolph called, relieved he knew what to do.

Snack-keeper Comet tossed up the slippery spread,
Along with a present. "The first one!" Santa said.

Blitzen slid down the chimney, the gift in her mouth,
Bringing Christmas cheer to at least one festive house.

"Thank you, thank you, Bobby!" the joyful reindeers cried,
As they leapt into the sky for their annual ride.
"We were lost and in need, and you helped us out,
And kindness is what Christmas is all about!"

Although Bobby arrived home dog tired and yawning,
He was as excited as ever on Christmas morning.
His new friends had left him a soft toy to play,
And a note which told him: "You saved Christmas Day!"

About the Author

Emily Benet is an author and illustrator.
She lives in Mallorca with her husband and two young daughters.
Her children's books feature her brother's Boxer dog, who was rescued from a rubbish (trash) bin and has become an online sensation.

You can read the book Bobby from the Bin (his origin story), watch his antics on social media and see Emily's online sketchbook by scanning the QR or following the links:
www.facebook.com/bobbyfromthebin   www.youtube.com/bobbyfromthebin

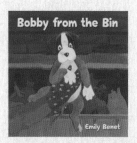

SCAN ME

Please write a review

Authors love hearing from their readers!
Please let Emily Benet know what you thought about this book by leaving a short review on Amazon or your other preferred online store.
It will really help other parents and children find the story!

Printed in Great Britain
by Amazon

32632694R00021